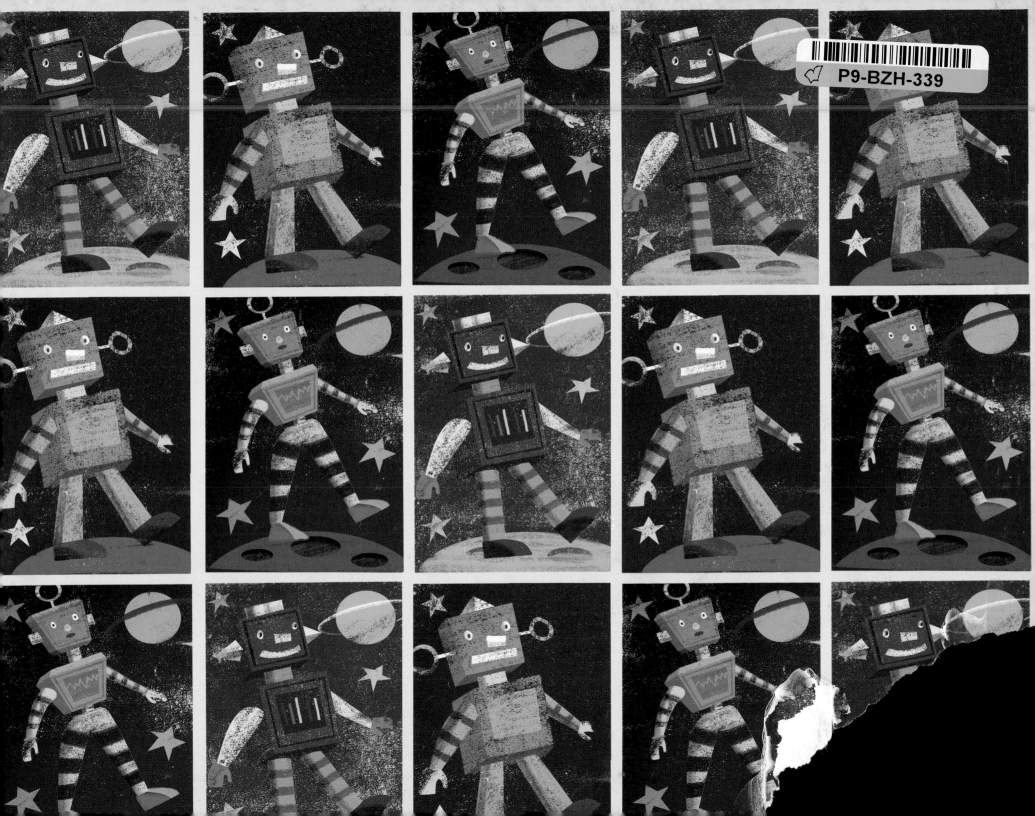

For Karen Grencik, my agent-bot
—M.P.

To P and TC, my two boys!
—S.M.

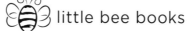 little bee books

A division of Bonnier Publishing
853 Broadway, New York, New York 10003
Text copyright © 2016 by Miranda Paul
Illustrations copyright © 2016 by Shane McG
All rights reserved, including the right of
reproduction in whole or in part in any form.
LITTLE BEE BOOKS is a trademark of Bonnier
Publishing Group, and associated colophon is a
trademark of Bonnier Publishing Group.
Manufactured in China   LEO 0316
First Edition   10 9 8 7 6 5 4 3 2 1
Library of Congress Cataloging-in-Publication Data
is available upon request.
ISBN 978-1-4998-0167-5

littlebeebooks.com
bonnierpublishing.com

Trainbots

by Miranda Paul   illustrated by Shane McG

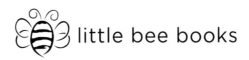

little bee books

Trainbots drawing, sawing, building.
Hammer, clamor, lots of gilding.

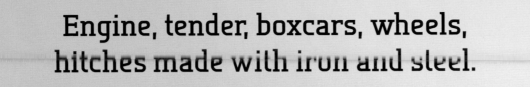

Engine, tender, boxcars, wheels,
hitches made with iron and steel.

Gears up front, caboose in back.
Station, platform, railway tracks.

Trainbots, ready?
Trainbots, steady?

Trainbots boarding, how rewarding!
Trainbots zooming, unassuming....

Badbots peeking, sneaking, scheming,
hopping, dropping—Badbots teeming!

Engine stopping,

hitches popping.

Now the train is flippy-flopping!

Trainbots scanning, planning, waving.

Must outsmart the misbehaving!

Trainbots drafting, engineering…

Clever crafting, rocketeering!

Flying, spying HERO-bots,
tying evil bots in knots!

Badbots sighing, crying, wailing—
HERO-bots are now prevailing!

Trainbots moving, grooving, driving.

Pretty soon they'll be arriving.

Packing, stacking, changing gear.

Chugga, chugga, choo...

Boybots, girlbots, kidbots cheering.
Brand-new TOYBOTS are appearing!

Toybots, ready?   Toybots, steady?

Kidbots screeching, reaching, swaying.
Tugging, hugging, time for playing!

Not just toybots to these kidbots—
these are FRIEND-bots 'til-the-end bots.